The Use of Shield Energies

By Patsy Stanley

ISBN 978-1-7326193-7-1

LCCN 2018908827

Studying metaphysics is a way of studying the whole of Life, using energy as the context.

All of Life is made up of the same energies.

Metaphysicians are learning the rules, the laws, so as to stay in line with them. To learn how to go with the universal flow…

This book is about Energy Shields, what they are, their uses, how to make them, and some of the reasons why we Hue–mans need them. The conscious use of energy shields can be very useful to protect and ingrain new strength and vitality into a depleted system, and works especially well for people who haven't had enough energy protection at one time or another throughout their lives.

Sometimes a Hue-man has a traumatic experience and feels that Spirit or God has let them down. They feel that God didn't protect them. Maybe it was Karma. No one knows all the answers. But that Hue-man can rest assured that the hierarchies that govern our lives were present, and knew about the event. We are never alone. Forget about why. Instead, transform your traumatic experience into power by building your shields consciously, which revitalizes your Hue-man self.

All cultures carry the ability to protect and renew themselves. All cultures have designated Sacred Protectors. Those Protectors and their hierarchies provide the energy combinations needed for protection in the particular area of life assigned to them.

Every culture has mythologies, stories, and rituals that revere their Protectors. All cultures rely upon their unseen Protectors in the invisible realms. A culture's spirituality relies upon their Protector myths to explain to them the energies they have to go up against. Those myths inform them about how to shape their weapons, build their homes, and what stances to take in their postures and with their relatives. The minerals, animals, rocks, plants, and all Matter that resides in the energy fields encompassing their area, become a part of their legends, stories, and traditions.

Let us take this information in another direction.

"As within, so without."

This wise old saying is the foundation of expressing our personal atomic structure as a Hue-man being. Everything comes from the inner self and expresses itself in the outer realms of form. What we manifest in the outer realms of form is a reflection of our inner self.

We are made of atoms. Every atom has a number of shells. Each shell is an atomic shield that shields that atom in some way. Every atom has a non-shielding outer shell, and an enlivening neon shell that allows for ether — Spirit — all vapors to enter. In human beings, as related to their soul and spirit bodies, these are the shields that connect Hue-mans to their divinity and the Divine Nature of all things.

Shielding is a natural part of our genetic coding. Our ancestors survived by learning to use specific shielding patterns for the different situations they encountered. They confronted life in specific patterns encoded into their DNA, just as we do today. Looking at our ancestral shield encoding will bring forth Heroes to emulate, Villains to be fought, and wrongs that need righting.
This is the adaptation process we participate in to ensure our progeny's survival on every energy level we have. In a larger framework, in some lifetimes we fight, in others we defend.

All shields use a combination of specific Motion and Matter with a specific Spin to it, to maintain its force.

When Motion and Matter get together, (Protons and Electrons) and create just the right amount of density, they create a shell or shield, that separates the before and after/time/speed (slower and faster) energies into their different vibrations and weights.

There are ancient Protector Myths from all over the world.

In the Angelic traditions found in most western cultures, the Archangel Michael is said to be the overall Protector of humanity on all of the energy planes. Michael works with the Fire Element, the highest in vibration of the four lower Elements.

In Hinduism, Shakti is the primordial Cosmic Energy, the Divine Mother Energy, and is the Protector of villages, cures diseases, punishes evil people, and gives welfare to the people.

In Japan, Hachiman is the Divine Protector. In ancient times Hachiman was agricultural. His symbol is a dove.

The learning of shields and their uses creates a stronger cellular structure within us. The ornate, intricate designs of shields, the fine manners, and High Speech are an outpouring of the Green Brotherhood Shieldsman's Stance. To make energy shields, use visualizations.

Who can use shields?

Anyone who has a need to can consciously use shields. One doesn't have to be bad or good to use shields. However, being good or bad DOES qualify one to work with specific Shields Masters.
Shields can be made out of anything you want to use.
Just be clear on what you need the shield for, and as to what you are going up against; don't forget the David and Goliath story.

Shields are generally used for protection, or to separate your energy from another. We make and use certain kinds constantly without ever thinking about it. Our cells protect themselves in this way, too.

Many times, we will make a shield so we can get clearer on who we are versus who they are, or to separate ourselves from harmful others or things. People automatically use shields when they are afraid of something specific to them or to all people in general so they can deal with it.

When we are scared, we build shields, consciously or not. People use colors, houses, and many other mundane things to make shields. Shields do not have to sacred. There are as many different kinds of shields as there are people.

It is best to work with shields in the early morning or evening. Don't spend a lot of time on them. Just a few minutes at a time. To keep a shield strong, visualize reinforcing the shield daily. As it becomes more solid, then go to it once in a while and check on it. Shore it up if it needs it. Remember it will stay in place until you take it down.
When building shields, always create a way to let the energy out that needs to go out, and create a way for the fresh energy to come in. You have to have both.
When you add density to the outer shell of the auric field around you, it becomes a shield. You do that visually. You can feel the weight.

If you decide to use a local area shield, you have to know where it is needed. You can test a shield with rock showers or hammer throws to see if it is strong enough. Visualize it. If it breaks, fix it.

Shields may be used to:

- ϖ Protect the physical body, including the Etheric double.
- ϖ Protect a Sensitive person in a crowd, or when they are having to be in many different energies.
- ϖ To protect the physical body while sleeping.
- ϖ For protection of others, more than for one's self.

- ϖ Use shields when sleeping in undesirable surroundings.

- ϖ Use shields to prevent danger of physical infection.

Thought forms make quick and handy shields in a crowd if one learns how to create them for air borne stuff. Just imagine a spray. People sending you negative energy at the office? Spray.

Protection in a crowd is twofold: Protection from energy you don't want, or that you don't want someone else to take on.

Energy Vampires

Use shields to protect forbidding emanations or vampire people. Vampire people are those who drain you of your energy. When they are done with you, all you can do is go away and sleep or go numb. Many times, you are unable to think coherently. They are usually very good at time warping. They learn early on how to steal time away from other people, as well as draining the electro-magnetic fluids from the person's Etheric web, causing a lessening of the joint padding and leaving the victim with other ailments such as emotional melancholy.

There are energy vampires in any large crowd. They are the people who are weak in some way, and who steadily drain copious amounts of vitality from the people around them. This activity mostly goes on without any of the parties involved, including the energy vampire, being consciously aware of what they are participating in.

These people are constantly absorbing every drop of specialized vitality-energy, they can get. If they confine themselves to the energy everyone throws out, no harm is done. Because that energy has already been received and dealt with by the person whose aura it is sucked from.

But as the vampire draws near, the usual outpouring is greatly stimulated by the vampire's drawing force, so that the energy already assimilated and accumulated or thrown out or released into the aura and hanging around there, is taken first, but then the intense suction begins to draw out the person's reserve of vital fluids and matter in only minutes. Anyone giving into this energy drain is making a mistake because these energy vampires almost always waste the energies they have acquired. They cannot properly assimilate the vitality, so it rushes through them, and their thirst is never slaked. It is akin to pouring water into a sieve. Energy vampires need to be given energy in strict and limited doses, and the elasticity of their Etheric double needs to be worked with to stop the leaks, which stops the need to suck energy. This leakage occurs through their whole body, not just through a tear or wound. This condition is indicated by their rigidity, and the lack of flow of fluidity in the Etheric double. When things get too rigid, they can break.

The In and Out

It is wise to learn how you can affect your inner being by doing things to help it, for then you have the two-fold ability to address both your distresses and happiness from the inner and outer realms of form.

Once you realize what that means, you become doubly powerful. For example, one could peel a basket of oranges and throw the rinds into one basket, and the whole orange into another, and it becomes a mirror of the inner and outer reflecting each other to help heal a brain tumor. Healing from the outer may not look exactly sane sometimes to those who don't know that the bodies all have to participate in any process. Certainly, it can look uncomfortable to many.

 Simple is sometimes the hardest to believe in. But it works, for I and many others have used these spontaneous processes and are witnesses to the positive, long term healings that working from the outer in an obvious way to mirror the inner, can bring.

Having this knowledge and claiming it, allows one to take an action on our own behalf or for someone else; an action that may look very silly, but is enough of an Outer reflection of what's going on in the Inner to make the healing happen.

Chemicals and pills can only do so much. You can take silly, simple, powerful, remedial actions yourself to remedy many things. Don't give up all your power to the current medical idea of over medicating people, especially our Elders and children.

You don't have to know everything to do it, either. All you have to do is do it. It is an instinctive art that everyone has. And it can and will help your inner condition.

This is the secret to a great amount of healing! Children know all about this. They know to get the time right and the place and stuff, and how to make the necessary adjustments. Many times, after all is in place, it takes only a minute or two for the healing to happen. Children are outstanding at helping other children heal negative emotional content. I have seen it done many times while people scoffed at the simplicity and the silliness of it, and chose to keep their own illnesses before they would allow themselves to be a Child, a Cosmic Clown, or a Fool, or to be led or advised by one in this role.

The roles of the Clown, the Fool, and the Jester are doorways to health and life. Those roles are doorways that allow the unseen healers access for passing along needed information through the spontaneous, intuitive psychic circuits that open in you when you take on one of these roles. There are people who grew up being allowed to keep these psychic circuits open and others who shut them down. But those circuits will open for anyone who is willing to step into the role of a "Silly Healer."

Principle

Shields should be used for protection. And for protection of others more often than for protection of oneself if you are lucky. Our helpers use shields frequently as defenses against certain influences when working with human beings.

The membranes of each cell of our body receives healthy, strengthening benefits from us knowing about Outer

Shields, and how and when to use them in the Outer Realms of Form, for this is working outside of the body to strengthen the cellular levels inside the body. "As within, so without" again. More symbolism becomes involved and is added in shield making as more facets arise.

Historically, this form of outer protection mirroring the inner protection, showed up externally in Medieval times when the people were trying to pull themselves up and out of the dark ages into a higher living energy.
Chivalry and the various forms of Honor and Courtesy were a way of keeping the higher, desired energies constant, the purpose being, so that the energies would not lower in vibration ever again into another Dark Age.
Jousting and the use of shields were a way to change the dark energies in the physical realms so the people could evolve. The coats of arms and their symbols, may have warned everyone ahead of time what the cell was capable of, (its intention) where it belonged and its genetic ancestry. This was the intentional Outer modeling of the interior of the person.

This energy shift came about through the Green Brotherhood, which is the home of the Shield Masters. All Shield Masters work through the Green Brotherhood and the Kingdoms associated with it.

Those methods are still in practice today, and still available. The Pagan community is consistent in carrying these practices forward. Their honoring of those methods with their traditional dress and actions gets the attention of the unseen Energy Beings that work with these energies, and honors them so that they might be renewed and gain their strength back. Circles are popular with Pagans, because the unwanted energy runs around and around the circle, and since there is no end, it wears itself out.

It might be wise to keep this in mind when you need help. Who knows, you may devise a successful way to help yourself or another into a more protected place.

Healers

Healers, shields are to be put in place before working with healing someone. You don't want your energy to get mixed up with theirs so that you take it on and process it for them. Your energy might be lower than theirs, in which case, you could cause them to get worse instead of better. So Healers, pay attention to your energy levels and your shields when you are helping someone. Get familiar with your energy and its levels and learn how to keep it good.

Sympathy energy can hold someone where they are. Compassion allows movement. The degree of the healer's investment in "fixing" it directly affects and supports the rise or decline of spontaneity in the process. Get over your investment in the outcome and let the energy do its work.

Energy is hard to work with when it is resistant to the flow. Energy tracks are created as energy flows. Keep this in mind when you work with people or other beings. The rule you have to follow is to ask permission from the person to work on them. If you feel "NO" coming from them, then don't do the work.
If you give someone else your energy, and take on their Karma, just know that it is much harder to get rid of someone else's Karma, because they have different vibratory rates throughout their systems than you have in yours.
Specify that the energy is coming from the universe to the person. The important thing is to ask the Beings who work

with them to come and assist them in the highest good of all. If the Beings who assist them say no, then stop. When healing, work with the Karmic lesson to be learned. That way, they and you must be specific about what can be done.

Stay neutral. Keep the result you want out of it. Look over the different stark bodies- see their bodies-the physical, Etheric, astral, mental. Look for the plane the disease is manifesting on, and deal with where that illness is, and work only with that.

Always create ways to let the energies come in and go out, negative and positive. When the healer is trying to cure, and is pouring strength into the person to be healed, inevitably, along with the vitality, goes a bunch of your own energy along with it. Mental and astral diseases can be conveyed to another this way, unless you learn to use shields.

When you work with healing somebody with your hands, always put a shield through your wrists. Concrete, stone, or gold is good, and see the shield going through your wrists so that you're not going to take in the person's energy and incorporate it into your own systems.

A lot of healers do not use shields, so they end up drawing in the person's energies or ailments. Don't give someone else your energy. There are tons and tons of energy available in the universe. Direct their energy needs towards that. We are just a tiny particle in the universe and don't need, and can't use that much of the energy. Begin learning to bring the energy in from the universe. See beams of energy coming from the universe, the sky, from outer space.

Beams are good to use to work with other peoples' energy. Use a karmic statement so you do not create more Karma for yourself, and so that you do not draw in their Karma and have to carry it out. Because their Karma is on its way down into manifestation and it must manifest somewhere, and it doesn't care where. You can willingly or inadvertently take on their karma. Once it lands, there is no giving it back or to someone else. You must process it. Much is to be learned about family curses and how they are passed on to consciously unaware participants. State that the person will be healed in accordance with their highest Karmic good, and the highest Karmic good of all, before you begin.

If you do this, the person will not get what they are not ready for, and what they have not earned the right to have. It is not unusual for a healing to be stopped because all the lessons from the illness have not yet been learned. And, it may have taken years to set up the situation they are in, so if you rush in and rescue them, they may be mad at you because they will have to set the whole thing up again to get their lessons from it. If the experience of the issue is still needed along their path of growth, do not get in the way of that. Let it go.

Another reason that you don't want to give someone your energy, is that yours may be more negative than theirs. You may be very negatively polarized, so why give someone that is sick more negativity that they already have?

Types of Shields

Time shields give time travel capabilities and futuristic capabilities. There are pulsating shields, permanent shields and temporary shields in these realms. All time shields apply the sound energies to get the job done. Physical Shields: things commonly used as physical shields: The obvious ones are houses, clothing, sunglasses, pulled shades, fences, locked doors.

In the physical, you can work with steel, rock, earth and all kinds of woods. Molten lead and tempered steel are two of the most powerful shields. Steel shields are good around cars- layer it with 3" steel-put it up with sound effects. Lead is good for shielding in plants- esp. nuclear - to prevent neg. energy from getting to you.

Red:
Lots of times, people use the color red to shield the physical body because red works with the physical body. You can visualize yourself inside of a red basketball. Spinning shields add power. Left to right spinning shield spins energy away. Right to left spins energy in. A Red Capsule shield has more electrical energy than the red basketball shield, but otherwise is the same.

Plants
Plants around the house, inside and out, and different kinds of trees, edible plants, medicinal plants such as Anjelica, betony, dill, rowan, and holly, to name a few can be used as shields. A few of a long list of herbs that can be as shields are mallow, mullen, mugwort, garlic, and onions.

Solomon's Seal shields both the aura and the physical body, and is useful for trauma.

Use Yarrow for protection against someone who drains energy. Wear a small pouch of it somewhere on your person.

Plants are here to care for us and feed us and all else. Plants are one of the ways the Earth provides sustenance for us. The more highly evolved the plant, the more highly evolved the Devas that work with them. Which is what gives the plant the animated effect. Plants outside the house- geometric form has lots to do with mental energy.

Plants are magnetic; the Devas working with them are electric. Climbing vines are among the most evolved of plants. It is said that plants only see plants and animals. They don't see inanimate objects. Red is a favorite color of plants.

Incense can be used to dispel negative vapors but use it very sparingly, or it will attract even more negative entities and thought forms. Do not use oils or scented candles, oils. There are a lot of junk oil and candle and heavily scented products out on the market these days that shouldn't be there. They hurt the respiratory system, affect all of the energy systems negatively, and call in negative energies that cling to us. Many illnesses arise out of using them. Oils and scented things are to be used only by those who understand what happens and are trained in the art of, and know the repercussions of, their use.

Different shields work with different elements that affect and work with different parts of the self.
- ϖ The Earth Element works with the physical body
- ϖ The Water Element works with the astral body.
- ϖ The Air Element works with the mental body.
- ϖ The Fire Element works with the soul body.

Gemstones

Gemstones can be used as shields because they work with the energies of separation. Faceted gems have more power. The more facets, the stronger the gem is.

Some gemstones protect by shielding one from harm, from the soul body on down. Other gemstones protect specific areas of the bodies, or specific bodies, and yet others protect from the mental, or the astral planes on down.

A few examples of the type of protection stones offer are:
- ϖ Spiritual protection - amethyst crystals
- ϖ Personal protection - black onyx
- ϖ Red soul plane protection - Rubies
- ϖ On the yellow soul planes - ivory, coral
- ϖ On the orange soul planes - pearls
- ϖ On the green soul planes - malachite-emeralds
- ϖ On the blue soul planes - opals
- ϖ Indigo and violet carry the fastest vibration energies humans have, and they are attuned to sapphires and diamonds.
- ϖ Use turquoise for astral or emotional protection.

The most powerful gemstones on this planet are usually the most expensive ones. Stones are sometimes used for decorating shields, and sometimes they are shields in themselves, depending on the stone. Humans have created myths about special stones since their beginning.

- ¬ Jewelry, in the way it is made, can be a shield.
- ¬ Opals empower the color energy blue.
- ¬ Amethyst crystals hold energy for a long time.

Cleaning Your Gemstones

Visualize a box around your gemstone. See beams of the appropriate energy going into it. The energy is self-selective. Just watch it and go with it. Program a timer into the box system, a timer that pulls in energy, and releases the power from the material in the gemstone once a day.

The Polarity, or electric and magnetic properties of a few gemstones:
- ϖ Opal-magnetic
- ϖ Emerald-highest green + - energy
- ϖ Ruby-magnetic.
- ϖ Garnet- magnetic
- ϖ Diamond- indigo- electric
- ϖ Star sapphire-indigo- electric and magnetic

Diamond and Star Sapphire are both good for third eye work. They are good for sight and hearing because both are soul energy stones. Yellow gold helps focus, and puts force behind what's going on.

Understanding Karma

Shields were created to separate vibratory levels, such as planets, universes, solar systems in space. Shields separate one from negative energy environments. Shields change morphic fields which are units of form arrangements of any size.

Energy moves in two basic ways. Energy moves from higher levels down into lower levels, and from lower levels back up into higher levels.
The energies moving down, by law, carry the intention and purpose of manifesting itself. That energy is moving **down**

into matter, which means it is going to take on some sort of form on one or the other planes of existence in our reality, and it is going to keep moving on down as far as it possibly can.

Be very careful about taking on someone else's Karma, their stuff coming down. You can act as a stand in for their Karma and get yourself crushed. Some people have illnesses and other things they may have set up karma wise, that took years in the planning. If you take it on, they may get off scott free and go off and have a good time while you die off. So, stay out of the way of Karma. Your own is enough, because Spirit is still the boss of us all and is running the Karmic part of this show too.

Another reason we move our energies downward, is to experience and understand the true connection to All That Is, to experience Organic Spirituality and gain the Organic Essences (fertilizers) necessary for our personal bodies, to connect and help others, and to carry out our and the universes Karma.

One of the reasons we move our energies upward is to strive towards both at-one-ment. The energy **moving back up** is entirely different, because that energy has a different purpose. And that purpose is to move out of manifestation, gradually releasing the balanced, distilled Essence of that part of life experiences in manifestation so it can be taken back up into the quickening God vibration.

The Word

The tongue and the sword are shaped alike. Both can be used for healing or hurt. Both are sacred and have power.

Your Voice is a weapon. Be careful about using your voice to attack another, it will come back on you. Lots of people do this, especially to children, and they don't know it. Just know that children are especially protected, no matter what happens to them. Many people just vent their negative emotions, and do not own them or take responsibility for dealing with them. They don't get that the negative, forceful energy is carried through their voice, and harms the other, whether the words do or not. Do it to children, and that's a ten times the energy back whammy.

Remember this principle before making a shield: When you speak about your shield, remember that the Word works with the throat chakra and puts the power behind it. Use your spoken Word, use it wisely to place magic and other powerful assets in support of your shields. That which we speak of puts power behind it. I hate - I love +. A war cry is a shield. A story about how this energy process works is Joshua and the battle of Jericho.

The Word works through the blue ray and the throat chakra. First, you think about it mentally. Then you visualize it on the astral planes where visualization takes place. Then you speak it in the physical. Be aware of this process in particular when speaking about your shields.

If you invoke the laws of Karma they will always manifest. To be safe, use the Word and state after making your shield, "Let this be done in the highest good of all concerned."

The Naming in the Book of Genesis in the Bible may be a group of stories about our genetics; stories about naming the DNA and RNA of our gene pools. This Naming process was about placing the power of the Word where it needed to be in the Beginning. The Naming process using the Word is both planetary, universal, and personal.

Manifestation and then release is the directed purpose of all energy processes. When energy is directed to a conceived end, it must go there.

Shields teach us how to best avoid or neutralize disturbing or undesirable energies or influences.

Be more concerned about density of shield than the size. It requires energy to build shields and maintain them. Shield energy work is done through visualization. When learning about shields, use more solid things to make them of, for example, oak instead of balsam, steel instead of aluminum.

When using your shields, do not try to stop the flow of positive energy. Love is life, and we are a part of life.

Use the Elements to create shields because the Elements are the energies of Form. They provide for manifestation in the spiritual realms and all other places. You can learn to feel density with your hands if you practice it. First, practice on inanimate objects, then on animals, plants, people. Soon you will be able to tell where the energy is heavier or quicker by gathering information through your hands, which are two of your greatest teachers.

Close your eyes if too much information is coming in, or if your opinion of how it should feel is too strong, or close you can them just to concentrate. Use this new knowledge you gain in combination with your growing knowledge about colors and elements.

Don't use the usual physical measures of time and weight on other levels to get things done. They don't work as well there. You have to use things like clouds, vacuums, or lightning, things that work with more space and faster speeds as you go up through the bodies.

We make and use physical shields easily. It is just as easy to imagine and visualize them for our use on all our energy levels, whenever we need them. So, tend to yourself on the Energy planes.

Shields can be useful when we are changing our defense structures. Shields are different than defense structures in that:
1. We create them out of choice, not out of the original core level defendable survival techniques we had to learn, that we have continued to build on.
2. When the need for the shield is over, we can remove it easily.
3. Shields used for too long can become part of the defense structure. Or a person may become too defensive from the accumulation.

Always use shields on a temporary basis, and plan to take them down when you no longer need them. You want them to be mobile, ones that can be taken down, not set in concrete, like out of place in time belief systems that concretize quicker than anything else.

Shields are not there for the same reasons. They are created out of a conscious choice to address a need that is not part of your permanent defense system.

If you decide to change by doing more internal work on yourself, therapy or so forth, that kind of work is done on your defense systems

When you are making a shield, consider what it is going to do when you take it down. What will happen. The faster the vibration of the shield, the faster it will de-structure. The bigger it is, the more there is to de-structure and the slower it goes, the more taking into the womb of Earth goes on, which is where manifestation must go before it begins its upward journey.

Pay attention to the energy environment the shield will be used in when making it.

All we Need is Love

No one is in charge of our life except us, but we can confuse that by what we take on from those around us.

This planet is negatively polarized. Depression is a loss of energy due to negativity. We have to work with our own energy systems to get positive in, because negative energy is always self-destructive and always catches up with you. It eats itself away and must constantly be fed.

Positive energy, whether it is positively polarized to the electric or the magnetic, is a natural building force that is always expanding.

Negative energy always self-destructs. Not a bad thing. Not a good thing. That is just its job, by law.

Positive energy expands and restructures outside the self. That is its job. Therefore, shields are not about good and bad in your personal life. They are about protection.

The more we work on ourselves and grow, the less fear we have, therefore, the more we come from the energy we call love.

Light energy comes from the mental planes of energy. Love energy comes from the heart chakra, and is a blend of the positive light and dark forces-energies. Love energy is the most powerful force in the universe and a shield cannot keep it out. As we grow and learn more about what love is, we need less shields.

Particular fears are common to everyone. Negative energy has its purpose. It dissolves everything in creation. It connects the Outer to the Inner. It keeps things together. It maintains gravity.

Negative energies are necessary to keep the many varieties of energies together, the planet Earth for example.

Rays go off on tangential forces when energy comes around.

The following is a lawful energy process:

Energy runs in a straight line until it encounters something. At that point, its nature is to make a full circle and cut across its own path, creating a circle. All circles contain resonance, which are the sound energies that come into it.

Sound and Time are the movements that initiate the cause of manifestation. Energy exists. It always has, and we bring about the experiencing of the energies ourselves.

The law of Osmosis is stronger than shields, so keep an eye on your energy. Mind over matter? A higher step is energy over matter.

The Governance of the Shield Hierarchies

All shields work with the Green Brotherhood and the Earth element, along with the force of personal willpower. The Green Brotherhood personality is headstrong, emotional, tender hearted, and has lots of energy.

You can go to temples to learn about shields and all other things. Masters and Inner Guides are people who have gone on before you. Don't try to understand their time line. They may be as ancient as when the Old Moon ruled the Earth or younger than you, if they are one of the Protectors of the Future. It is always wise to listen to the little children.

Masters and Guides are not to be confused with Guardians. You can get in contact with them by being still and going inside yourself without distractions from the outer world.

Shield Masters and Energy Temples

Many Masters do more than one thing.

You must speak properly to the Guardians of the Temples, or they won't allow you access to anything in their domains. They don't have to. They don't need you, you need them. If you ask them to be your teacher, ask for what you truly are after.

Everyone has an inner guide who helps them along their path, to see that it goes as it has been chosen. These are beings who have mastered certain levels of information through their experience.

Learn your teacher's names. Learn the shield masters' names and what they do, and what area of expertise they cover. To find their names, ask to go to the proper temples and do your research.

Master Yuktiswar teaches about creation and the atom.

- ꙮ A mental shield temple to ask to learn at is - Sa-Ba-Ta.
- ꙮ An astral shield temple to ask to go to - Doranda-Jordante.
- ꙮ Lad-van a is a healing temple on the mental plane.
- ꙮ Sa Hearon Ka Day Ken Wal is spiritual city on the mental planes. It has connection city to the astral plane spiritual city of Shamballa.
- ꙮ Aura cleaning and shields - Ma ha ka han.
- ꙮ Ba Ba Gee –Avatar of the planet Earth, some say he is about 3000 years old, lives in the Himalayas.
- ꙮ Doranda – is a shield temple on the astral plane.
- ꙮ Mia Calani - is the astral temple of golden wisdom, of higher soul learning.

- Les Mi del Ma Say is the powerful pure white Snow Queen of Deimones. She is a Master who helps those who cannot go back and heal themselves emotionally, because the traumas (wounds) are too great. This Yin Master is seated before the Council of Mayferre and gives the Council guidance and directs the Council in their Due Diligence Process.

- Buuu Ru Meun Lao is the Master Leader of the Gland vibrations. To remove poisons from a gland, one must petition the Elementals He is in charge of.

There are different spiritual cities on all the energy planes. Shamballa is an astral temple, a spiritual city on the Etheric astral plane. Spiritual cities are located on the upper levels of each plane of energy.

Go meditate and talk to your own guides. You will have as many as you have chosen, or have chosen you. You will meet a lot of them in the temples when you go there. There are temples of learning, and of understanding, and of everything that needs to be known within the voids between certain levels.

About Those Levels

Everything, before it manifests on any other plane of existence as we know it, exists in a void, before it comes down. Between the physical level and the astral level, there is a void of the un-manifest.

Everything that manifests in the physical world, begins in the void of the un-manifest.

Within that void are temples of learning, understanding, peace, and all kinds of different things that one can tap into by their personal form of meditation, whatever that looks like for them.

There is a void between each level, and there are different temples on each level, and the specific Euchasic records for each level are held in these voids, in those temples.

There is more than one level for these records. The Euchasic records being the orderly recorded memory essences of our past lives pertinent to that area of Life experience. They are recorded and placed in the Causal Levels for that area of experience and expression.

The different Levels of Manifestation, physical, astral, mental and soul, the Spirit Goddesses, and the Photons in matter, surround all this. (The various Spiritual essences.)

How to go to Spiritual Temples

There is always a Master Guard that stands in front of every temple. They decide whether you can go in or not, based on your vibrations, because certain levels of information can be harmful to the uninitiated.

We go through levels of learning with our Masters by Initiation. There are different levels of initiation to protect us, and you can be given inner gifts, and outer gifts to achieve this end. Certain stones, a robe, other gifts, bracelets, amulets, and many other things can be given during an Initiation.

There is a big rush of energy during an Initiation. The time is spent joyously connecting the dots and having "ahas!" Many initiations take place during **Weisak,** which occurs yearly during spring when the full moon is in Taurus. This time is considered to be the beginning of the spiritual astral spring-time of the Spirit year. Weisak takes place in Shamballa, an astral spirit city. During Weisak, people go before the Boards and the Brotherhoods, and get a sort of report card on how they have been doing the past year.

Based on the report card, re-calibration of the person's energies takes place, Initiations are given to the people who have earned them, new teachers are assigned, feasts, dances and celebrations take place, and temples are readily available for many needs.

Most Shield Masters are also Energy Masters. Most Shield Temples work with Energy Temples. These temples offer all kinds of learning and ways to learn it. Just ask. Pretty soon, you will be led to your kind of study methods. Just ask to go to a temple, and they will tell you where, if you don't know. You don't need to know the name of it. But the plane of energy it is on dictates the preparation needed for the vibratory rate shift you will have to achieve or undergo in order to attend classes there.

Before entering, you will be put through a ritual of purification, usually involving water or bathing in a pool of blue water before you are allowed to approach a temple.

The Etheric is the energy double for the physical body. It is the upper level of the physical plane of energy. It is the un-manifest just before physical manifestation occurs. The Etheric web surrounds the aura. It is a gold fibered web-like bulb which begins at the base chakra and goes down and out and surrounds the aura. People who drink a lot or do a lot of drugs, prescription or otherwise, can get holes, rips, or tears in their Etheric web.

Blocked Energies

Colors and elements run through our body's meridians. When acupuncturists and massage therapists hit a sore spot, that's a blocked energy meridian. The energy has stopped there due to some experience in one's physical life or an experience in one of our other bodies. And the energy flow has been stopped. That's why, many times, they want the patient to go back and re-experience the event in some way, because it will break up the energy block.

Unwanted Sexual Energy

Lots of people throw sexual energy at other people without their permission. This is very rude, and indicates a need to learn to have better energy manners on the other planes of existence.

Most men, and some women, are not aware that they need to learn better energy manners on all the levels, in order to master the other levels of growth. Until they learn this, they don't have mastery of what they are working to gain.

Here is a shield to repel unwanted sexual energies.

Encase yourself in a large one inch thick red/violet (purifies energies) bubble, then make another bubble outside of that one you are in. Make it a dark blue and one inch thick, then start them spinning from left to right to repel. After spinning smoothly, place a mirror outside of them to ricochet the energy back to the sender.

For the sexual organs area of the physical body, use a blue water colored disc to cover them. Place the disc about four inches away from body, then spin left to right. Clockwise.

The Children

Never place shields right up against your body, but outside of your energy field, at least 2-3 inches between you and whatever it is you are saying "no" to.

Always build shields around and outside the Etheric web which is outside of the "aura'. Be careful to do this when building shields for children, too.

Help for the children:

Masters to call upon for the Children

The Greek Artemis and the Roman Diana were Protectors of the Vulnerable. Artemis took care of her mother without reward, and is a protector of children and childbirth, and can be petitioned to during the New Moon.

All of the Shield Masters are to be addressed respectfully. They will not, and are not obligated to help any Hue-man, unless that Hue-man has been assigned to them through the Mercy or Grace of one of the Residing Ether Elders.

However, the Hue-man Children's Masters may always be called upon for help for our children. Late at night when the Ethers are resting, or at dawn's break are the purest, strongest time to call upon them.

We can call upon these Masters to help our children.

- ϖ Mai Hana Yu works with transmuting the sadness.
- ϖ Bell Arch Kissae crusades for the children.
- ϖ Zi Mi Toe Yaster teaches Earthly tapping of Resonance.
- ϖ Eb beb eh eh Le works with the Breath of Life.

Let the children keep their natural smell because when the Masters helpers come to see what's going on, they must be able to smell the child's natural exudations because those smells contain the genetic coding information needed to send back to the Children Healers Temples. The smells are used to sort the animal and plant kingdom assistance needed. They will prompt you if a certain scent is needed.

We have the ability to accept or reject the energy sent to us. Children must learn this in order to grow up.

- ϖ Lack of Air element- mental disorders
- ϖ Too much air element - hyper-mental- never gets to the astral- astral never gets to play
- ϖ kids who stay around adults and don't get to be astral- if stay kids and don't grow, will need more air mentally-see body honeycombed with air blowing through-lung disorders- all breathing.
- ϖ Too much Fire- too much help
- ϖ headache or too much red- may be combination of both- don't overlook this- works with heart
- ϖ too much-fever- combat with magnetic energy- blue green, water element.
- ϖ Excess of electric energy can cause-fever-diarrhea-lots of nervousness –talk too much

For hyper kids- no red clothes, no dark colors or wild geometric patterns in anything, no psychedelic colors. Paint rooms in soft blues or greens, (no electric colors, no brilliant oranges, reds, pinks, or glaring yellows for example) stay in the middle with pale colors, soothing, change sheets to match, use natural materials, not micro fibers and such, put in medium blue bulb in night light- will sleep better.

You can teach your inner people something on the inner planes. Talk to them on the inner- use imagination- - explain what's happening; teach them to be helpful, they can take child to healing temples, to shield temples, energy temples, garden of the gods, wherever you are led, give to Master to deal with when stuck in "I don't know what to do or who to send to or to ask."

Send to Masters Lagattas or Regemos

Both these Masters work with astral plane healing for Hue-man children. They focus on healing the children. They work with color disorders. That means they heal father principle energies. They work with the color energies on the astral planes and the color Beings in astral matters.
They will check karmic records to see if it is appropriate to help person at this time. If it is not, they will send to other Healers to find who is needed at this time.
If you have a mother principle disorder, they will call in an Archangel helper on your behalf. They will ask him to help-are there for protection- are there to keep the child and you from getting lost.

Everyone has at least two guardian angels. Ask for their help. Get to know them before you need them.

Sick people or people who are on a lot of strong medications need serious shield protection provided for them by the people who have the extra energy to do it.

This can be easily done from any distance. Use prayer if the person is religious, for most religions have strong protection prayers.

Or you can visualize and ask the Masters for help for them.

Parents build shields for children constantly, they are necessary, and someone should do that for frail, aging, sick or disabled people.

Shields can be used to keep a person in their own energy field, so that they do not process another energy that may be inundating their energy field. Shields should be used for this purpose. Parents do this for babies and children all the time.

To disable negative energy, use the elements. See wind blowing through the aura, changing the vibration and rhythm. Ask Raphael, who is the Archangel of all the manners of healing, to help to pull out the negative energy.

Building Body Shields

Astral Shields

Use shields here to ward off undesirable emotional energies:

ϖ Pyramid shapes
ϖ Love is Pink

Use the water element. Use a tidal wave to wash out the negative. Stand in a clean, pure blue diamond shape. Use a blue diamond as an emotional or astral shield, spin it left to right. Helps force away unwanted energy.

On the astral planes, we have astral currents, what we call "fads" going on, because the elementals like to go along with the newest currents en masse. Like a school of fish in a water tank. Energy on the astral plane is undulating, like waves, those energies are soft. The astral body is a shimmering, iridescent color, full of vibrancy.

Joe and Ethel:

Astral energies, wants, desires, wishes, all move about on the astral plane. You can build useful little astral thought forms on the energy planes. Build one on each energy plane to get what you want. Give them names- such as "Joe and Ethel."

Visualize one on the left shoulder for the astral planes. Visualize the other one on the right shoulder for the mental planes.

Talk to the astral plane Pal. Tell them how they fit in your world. Tell them how they can help you out. Then tell them they are the ones for the job, they can get the job done.

Then talk to the mental plane Pal. It will help you to convince the mental body that it can understand and train for the job you need it to do. Tell it, "I have the right education and training- good planning- will be best to go for it- so will be one step ahead- are planning path for manifestation of what I want." Then watch how much help they become to you!

Mental Shields

ϖ Use to protect from unwanted thought energies.
ϖ Use the air element

Stand in a yellow triangle with a gold ball hovering above your head.

ϖ Love is rose on mental planes. Blushing
ϖ Love is gold on higher mental planes

ϖ Mental is stars which are combinations of triangles - also used for Cosmic protection - and from things such as metal poisoning. Mental body Masters work with the Air Element. There are many different kinds of Winds. Seek yours out and stand in it. Listen to it. If you are able to hear and listen, it will give you the name of the Master you seek if you ask wisely, with respect and cleanness.

ᛒ The triangle protects mental energies.

ᛒ The gold star is a high mental shield. The five-5-point star works with the power of projection. If you want peacefulness and tranquility, use the 6 –six-point star.

Mental energy is electric- can easily turn into jagged energy.
If you are doing a lot of mental work, like office work or studying, then make a big gold or yellow ball and place it above your head. Have a beam of energy coming down from it, refreshing and supplying your mind with new energy constantly as needed, and you will think easier, and be able to be mentally on track much longer.

You can use blue, for it is calming, which allows more flexibility on the mental planes. The mental energies get more and more rigid and into rote as they get used up. Blue makes them flexible again.

Visualize releasing excess energies (maybe heaped on you by a coworker or other) by seeing yourself step through a plexiglass shield.

You come through clean, the unwanted energies, whether good or bad, stay in the plexiglass and disappear through a small four-inch-wide fan spinning clockwise in the top of the shield.

Keep these energies around you, so people who need, will take energy from these sources instead of taking from your own personal energy.

You can use shields when working in business or school to block out noise, energy flows, and outside forces. Place one of the new digital photo frames on your work desk and fill it with pictures of nature. Always create shields to achieve this type of serenity in a big space, such as outdoors, then carry the shield back with you to use in the cities or office.

Use them when you are on vacations, in parks or other places, to prevent getting energy you don't want. This shield brings balance on the green and blue planes of energy. Puts you back in harmony, or in balance, which is harmony. Also, good to use in hyper-business situations. It is soothing to the body. Blue and green energy is cooling and healing to stop noise irritation.

Don't give your power away due to programming- parents-expectations-churches, and don't get caught up in negatives.

Soul Shields
- ϖ Use to protect from unwanted soul energies.
- ϖ To protect all the bodies, use a blue-violet amoeba shape that is constantly moving and changing. Place all the bodies inside of it.
- ϖ Love is lavender
- ϖ Use the fire element and Amethyst crystals.

Not centered or can't seem to stay centered? If you set your shields in place on the soul levels, the energy will filter down. Soul shields help to center the self and align the bodies all the way down.

Rose- works with the low causal planes- deep rose violet magenta, Indigo for the low soul planes, Violet for the high soul planes

Physical Shields

- ω Use squares of earth for physical protection.
- ω Triangles
- ω Love is a rainbow
- ω

You can use:

- ω Walls
- ω Mirrors
- ω Cubes
- ω blue clouds
- ω Red for physical shields

Make a ring of mustard yellow, onyx black, and chestnut brown. Spin it to the right. Use as a shock or violence absorber. Place a ring of it around your car or yourself when walking in an undesirable location. This shield also works well in loud noise situations. It is good for noise sensitive people to learn to use this particular shield because it works well in loud music situations.

To get an energy shield to manifest, surround it with earth-it will help pull it down.

A Gentle Shield: The Fractured Mirror

A fractured mirror sends fractured energy back. It takes longer to connect back to itself and is a gentler way to return the energy to its sender.

Green adds balance to any environment and any situation.

Dead or alive, we are constantly having a Relationship with this living planet, the universe, the galaxy, the moon, the sun, all other planets, and to all others because energy never dies, it simply changes its form time after time...

A Grounding Technique:
Here is a simple and quick grounding technique that works. Visualize yourself standing barefoot on the Earth. Quickly dive down into the earth as if into a pool of water, and go down and down until you reach the beautiful, red brick colored clay earth.

Touch the clay and then come back up through the earth as you would swim up through water. Then, standing on the earth once again, feel the personal cleanliness and the grounding you are experiencing. Feels great, doesn't it?

Cleansing the Emotions:
To cleanse the emotions, picture a five-foot-tall, maybe three-feet wide small cave with a rock ledge over the top of it. This flat slab of three-inch-thick rock has water tricking over it and pouring down in front of the cave, creating a small place to stand under it in the water's mist. The rock can change to a crystal if you need to cleanse the mental

body. Or to turquoise for astral protection. You can change the sound of the water, its speed, or the sounds, and you may close the cave if you wish. You'll know what to do for you. You can do this visualization any time, but it is most powerful at dusk or dawn.

A fun and quick energy cleansing technique:
Here is a fine cleansing technique for unloading old stuff, or stuff that isn't yours, or that is negative junk weighing you down, that you don't want any more and want to get rid of. This one is particularly good for removing the stress of hauling unwanted negative loads of energy around forever.

See and hear a big garbage truck coming from off in the distance. It is coming down out of a low, cloud bank and maybe down a hill. You suddenly understand that the truck can haul off all your unwanted stuff that you don't need to hang on to any more. You know, the stuff you were holding on to, to make sure you're were getting your karma right. Junk that you have been hanging on to without realizing it on every level. All the negative junk you throw into the back of the truck will be taken away.

 So, get those big black garbage bags and get busy filling them up! You haven't got long. When the garbage truck gets there, haul the garbage bags to the truck and toss them into the back of it.

The garbage truck stays briefly, and then moves off into the distance and out of sight. It is taking the negative energy to be cleaned up and recycled so it can be given out again.

You will see the other people laughing and throwing their garbage bags in the back of the truck. You might see other people unloading their black trash bags into it that you don't know. The truck will come around again for pickup, but it does not come at your beck and call. Pretty soon, if you pay attention, you will become aware of the truck's schedule and take advantage of it.

To Recharge the Self: A Shields Meditation

Sit down, relax, and close your eyes. Imagine yourself sitting on top of your favorite hill or mountain. The sun is shining. The mountain can be anywhere you choose, like the Rockies, or the Cascades, or the Appalachians. It is a place where the air is pure and clean, where the vibrations are much higher than they are down in the city.

Look around the valley below. Put a little creek running down the middle of the bottom of the valley. Look at all the different kinds of trees. Hickory, pine, some oaks, cedars. Maybe there are animals on the other side of the stream.

There may be deer, beavers, squirrels, rabbits, and all kinds of birds. Take in the green of nature, and the red of the earth. Take in the sunlight and the yellow and blue of the sky.
Let yourself drift down to the water's edge. You can walk or float down to it. Lay down in the water so that it is coming through from the head and washing out through your feet.

Let the water flow through your body. Feel the magnetic coolness of the water. Relax and let it pull out all of your worries and troubles and all of the negativity you have built up. Let it pull out the tension you've built up today.
Feel the water pouring through your body, your muscles and bones, and touching every single pore of your being.

When you are finished, rise calmly out of the water. Look off in the distance. See a storm coming. As the storm gets closer, a rainbow forms.

A strong clear red is on the top. Then orange, yellow, green, blue, indigo, and then violet on the bottom. Step out of the water and drift towards the rainbow. It is coming closer and getting bigger. Step into the rainbow.

You know all about rainbows. You love them. You are wise. You know that you have to walk faster through the colors red, orange, indigo, and violet than you do the other colors.

First, red. Feel the energy flowing through you. It gives you strength and courage and more will power. Then step into orange and feel its energy for a moment. You are gaining more love, unity and wisdom.

Step into yellow and feel the energy. Let it pull out the negative yellow energy and replace it with positive. Now your thoughts are clear and positive and objective. Then step into green. Green works with balance.

Let the negative energy go and feel it being replaced with positive energy. Feel it flowing from the top of your head, all the way down through your body and out your feet. You are balanced with yourself and the world.

Now step into blue. Blue works with peace. Feel it calming you as it flows down through your body and out your feet. Feel the old tensions release and flow away. The world is in harmony.

Now step into indigo. Stepping into indigo is always a purification ritual. It is blue-violet in color. Feel it passing through your third eye as it travels down through your body.

You can see and hear everything better.

Quickly step into violet. Feel it breaking up the dross and removing it from your system. Feel it strengthening the meridians and the Etheric web. You are becoming more spiritual all of the time. Step out quickly, do not linger in violet.

Now, step out of the rainbow. See the clouds drift off into the distance. Drift back up to your mountain top. Sit down and look at the world again. See if looks and feels any different.

Take a moment and thank Nature for being there and for all of its natural beauty and its place in our being. Then slowly, come back into the room, and back into your body. Open your eyes when you are ready. Don't hurry.

We are living 'neath the great Big Dipper
We are washed by the very same rain
We are swimming in the stream together
Some in power and some in pain
We can worship this ground we walk on
Cherishing the beings that we live beside
Loving spirits will live forever
We're all swimming to the other side

I am alone and I am searching
Hungering for answers in my time
I am balanced at the brink of wisdom
I'm impatient to receive a sign
I move forward with my senses open
Imperfection, it will be my crime
In humility I will listen
We're all swimming to the other side

On this journey of thoughts and feelings
Binding intuition, my head my heart
I am gathering the tools together
I'm preparing to do my part
All of those who have come before me
Band together to be my guide
Loving lessons that I will follow
We're all swimming to the other side

When we get there we'll discover
all the gifts we've been given to share
have been with us since life's beginning
and we never noticed they were there.
We can balance at the brink of wisdom
Never recognizing that we've arrived
Loving spirits will live together
We're all swimming to the other side.

'We are Swimming to the Other Side'

1992 Pat Humphries

Moving Forward Music BMI